# The Zombie Whisperer

## and Other Weird Tales

Steven E. Wedel

This is a work of fiction. Any resemblance to real people, living or dead is purely coincidental or used fictitiously.

**MoonHowler
Press**

ISBN: 0692399135
ISBN-13: 978-0692399132

# DEDICATION

This book is dedicated to the rednecks, the hillbillies, and the trailer trash who know better than to overthink a problem that requires a physical solution.

ALSO BY STEVEN E. WEDEL

## Novels and Novellas

Inheritance

Little Graveyard on the Prairie

Seven Days in Benevolence

After Obsession (with Carrie Jones)

Amara's Prayer

## Collections

Darkscapes

Unholy Womb and Other Halloween Tales

The God of Discord and Other Weird Tales

## The Werewolf Saga Series

Call to the Hunt

Murdered by Human Wolves

Shara

Ulrik

Nadia's Children

## As Editor

Tails of the Pack

# CONTENTS

# ACKNOWLEDGMENTS

"One Night in Benevolence" was originally published in the Amazon Shorts program in 2006. "The Zombie Whisperer" was first published in *Dead Set: A Zombie Anthology* (2010) by 23 House. "Dead Betty" and "Noodlers Nab Nekkid Nymphs" are new for this collection.

# THE ZOMBIE WHISPERER

Jana Wikel heard Ken enter the room behind her, but she didn't turn around to greet him. She sat mostly still, staring at the citizen's band radio, waiting for a reply while she gently tapped the microphone against her pursed lips. Behind her, Ken shifted his weight from foot to foot. He smelled of sweat and gunpowder.

"You say the zombie is your father?" The voice from the radio was clipped and curt, an upper East Coast accent. Jana wondered why the man was in Mobile, Alabama, with that accent.

"That's what I said," Jana answered, suddenly very aware of her own Deep South drawl.

"Can you afford Dr. Dragoon's services, Miss Wikel?" the man asked. "You've gathered the items we discussed last week?"

"Yes," Jana answered.

"You shouldn't do this," Ken interrupted at last. Jana continued to ignore him.

"Dr. Dragoon can be there tomorrow morning," the radio man said.

"You've got the directions," Jana reminded. "Land your helicopter on the lawn on the south side of the house.

They can see you on the north and it excites them."

"You said the area has been cleared," the radio man accused.

"What I said is that we clear the area daily," Jana answered. "That takes a while. New ones come during the night. Every night." *Every fucking night!* "We shoot them during the day. They can't get in. We haven't had one break through in six months."

"Eight," Ken corrected. "Lance let those two in six months ago."

"Whatever," Jana said. She remembered. "Make that eight months," she said into the mic.

"Good," the radio man said. "Our ETA will be 9 a.m."

"See you then," Jana said. "Over and out." She put the microphone down. Behind her, Ken's military boots clomped across the tiled floor. Jana covered her eyes but noted the sounds of Ken pulling a wooden chair up to the table to sit facing her.

"You know this is bullshit," he said.

"I don't," she answered. "And neither do you."

"Oh, I know it's bullshit," he said. "It's level after level of bullshit. We've got a pretty good thing here. Your daddy built a wall around his big house and it keeps those things out, but that wall fucked with your mind, Jana. You're too sheltered. You don't know what it's like out there."

"No." Jana couldn't completely suppress the shudder.

"You're hiding in here."

"We're all hiding in here," Jana said.

"Most of us are hiding because we know what's out there," Ken said. "You're just hiding from the truth."

Jana dropped her hands to the table and faced him at last. Ken hadn't shaved that morning. His chocolate cheeks and sharp chin were rough with short black-and-gray stubble. The short-sleeved denim shirt he wore was already stained with sweat and gore. *It was a busy morning.* Jana pulled her gaze from a smear of crimson and gray at his shoulder and was caught by his eyes again. They were hard, dark eyes, but there was more there ... maybe love, maybe sad resignation.

"I have to do it," Jana whispered. "If he can tell me, I have to know. Wouldn't you do the same?"

The question broke the spell Ken's eyes had been conjuring. He looked away quickly, sighed, and stood up. The 9mm pistol at his side seemed incredibly black and square as he moved, then he was behind her and his giant, hard hands were on her shoulders, rubbing away the tension.

"They don't understand shit, Jana," Ken said. "They're dead. The soul, if such a thing really exists, is gone. They ain't who they were. I've come to terms with it, and you should, too."

"Not yet."

"This guy you're bringing in here," Ken continued. "We don't know anything about him. They come in here with guns and who knows what, find out there's only four of us, and they might just clean us out. If we're lucky, they might shoot us in the head before they leave."

"They won't."

"How do you know that?" Ken asked. He stopped massaging and returned to his chair. "You don't. All you know is that shit you heard on the radio. A fucking CB radio advertisement. You talked to anybody he's helped already?"

"Yes," Jana said, perking up. "Before I ever talked to his people. I talked to a woman down in Savannah and she said Dr. Dragoon helped her."

"How do you know that woman was in Savannah?" Ken asked. "She could have been sitting on Dr. Dragoon's dick for all you really know. The CB radio ain't no better than those Internet chat rooms were. You don't know who you're really talking to."

"I trust her," Jana said.

"You're still living in your daddy's walls," Ken said, but his voice wasn't harsh.

"I have to try," Jana said. "If you're right, fine. I'll start going to the stands with you guys. I'll shoot zombies with you. I'll help you drag the bodies to the fire. But right now, I can't. Not while I believe there's still some spark of humanity in them."

"All right, baby. All right." Ken stood up, leaned over and they kissed briefly. Jana's nose recoiled at the smell of gunpowder, smoke and human gore on his shirt, but she held the kiss, nipped his tongue when he tried to put it into her mouth, then pulled away, smiling.

"You stink," she said.

"Yeah. Tom and Lamar already hit the shower. That's where I'm heading. Join me?"

Jana thought about it for a moment, then agreed. She held onto his arm as they moved through the mansion's lower floor toward the biggest bathroom.

"Philosopher Tom don't seem to care about us," Ken said, "But it drives Lamar crazy that you're doing me and not him."

"He should find his own woman," Jana joked, then she remembered Lance and the joke wasn't funny anymore.

\* \* \*

"Everything's ready?" Jana asked. Her eyes were fixed on the buzzing dot approaching the mansion from the south.

"Honey, it's as ready as it can be," Ken answered.

"I know. Sorry," Jana said. They watched the helicopter from one of the twelve freestanding deer stands set up along the 10-foot-high brick wall surrounding the mansion. Below her, on the other side of the thick wall, two dozen zombies in various stages of decay moaned and reached hungrily toward them. Jana tried very hard to ignore their cloudy eyes, rotting flesh and grasping hands. Ken seemed to sense her discomfort.

"This is what they are. No humanity. They're like sharks, except they don't shit. They just eat and make more like them," he said.

"Where's Lamar," Jana asked. Gaunt and bearded, Tom stood on another platform to her right.

"Listen, Jana, we gotta play this cool," Ken said, his voice deadly earnest. "I got Lamar set up somewhere to keep an eye on these jokers' helicopter. We're gonna make them believe Lamar was killed, so they think we're down to three."

"But that's just — "

"No, Jana. This is the way it is. This is your place and for the most part I let you run it your way. But I've been out there. I grew up in the ghetto and I've seen what people, not just poor people, but everyone, what they've become since all this shit happened. You can't trust nobody, Jana. You play along when I say Lamar was killed last night. If these people are for real — or at least not here to rob and kill us — it won't matter that they never see him.

If they try to fuck with us, he's our ace in the hole. And that ain't much. Look at that." He nodded toward the approaching helicopter. "Blackhawk. Bet you thought they'd show up in some old tourist chopper, huh?"

Jana didn't answer. She suddenly felt uneasy about the approaching military helicopter. Ken took her by the arms and made her look him in the eyes.

"It'll probably be fine," he said. "But be ready, just in case."

Jana nodded. "I will. Let's go."

They hurried off the stand and rushed toward the grassy lawn at the end of the swimming pool. The men had spray painted a circle in the grass with a big H in the center. Looking close, Jana noted there were uneven seams in the grass where it appeared to have been carefully dug up and replaced.

"You mined the landing area?" she asked.

"Yep."

"I hope I'm right," Jana said. "I can't stand the thought of living in a world where you have to suspect everybody of the worst."

Ken gave her a sidearm hug. "The world has always been like that. You white bread rich folks just didn't know it." He smiled as he said it, but Jana was irritated at his constant reminders of her former wealthy status.

"I just hope you're wrong," she said, then the ominous black helicopter descended onto the explosive circle and further conversation was drowned out.

As the engine shut down, three men hopped out of the helicopter. Two were massive, muscular black men, heavily armed, wearing sunglasses and black jumpsuits. They seemed even more gigantic when compared to their lean companion, a mustachioed man with an angular face, dark hair and pale skin. The white man wore a charcoal gray suit, minus the tie, and appeared unarmed. He stepped forward, his hand outstretched to Jana.

"Miss Wikel," he yelled in greeting.

Jana nodded and shook the hand as the propeller blades finally quieted, then became still. "Dr. Dragoon?"

"At your service, ma'am." He offered a low bow, then straightened and fanned his face effeminately.

"Would you like to come inside?" Jana asked.

"That would be fantastic," the doctor agreed.

They started forward, the two armed men following their leader. Ken didn't move. "Your other two men coming in?" he asked.

Jana looked from Ken to the helicopter, where an average looking white man sat behind the controls. Another black man, not so muscular but also in a black jumpsuit, loitered near a Gatlin gun mounted at the chopper's open side door.

"No, they'll stay with the helicopter," Dr. Dragoon said.

Jana caught the look Ken gave her and bit her lip. "That's fine," she said. "Let's get out of this heat."

As they were about to enter the front door of the stone house a rifle shot rang out. Dr. Dragoon's men reached for the automatic rifles strapped on their backs, but a motion from the thin white man stopped them. He looked questioningly at Jana, but it was Ken who spoke.

"That's Tom," he said. "He's clearing visitors on the north wall. Maybe your men could give him a hand?"

9

"Oh no," Dr. Dragoon said. "Andrew and James are quite necessary to me. They subdue the fleshly prison of the *spiritus* so that communication can take place."

"Uh-huh," Ken said.

"Not a believer, I see," Dr. Dragoon said, smiling. "We'll change that."

Another gunshot rang out and Jana led the group into the house. There was no air conditioning; that would have put too much strain on the generators in the garage. Ceiling fans stirred the humid air above them, the whir of the motors interrupted by the sound of the men's boots on the hardwood floor.

"There's only the three of you now?" Dr. Dragoon asked.

"That's right," Ken said quickly. "Lamar was careless yesterday. We lost him getting your payment."

"I'm very sorry," the doctor said. "He was a close friend?"

"He was alive," Ken said.

Jana led them to a room near the back of the house, beyond the library. She stopped before a heavy, solid wood door. "This is it," she said. "Daddy's in there."

"He's alone?" Dr. Dragoon asked.

Jana nodded, keeping her face blank. "He ... he followed me in there and I ran out and closed the door. He's been in there ever since."

"How long did you say?"

"Two months. He died of pneumonia."

"It's a pity most of our doctors were among the first killed when the apocalypse began," Dr. Dragoon said.

"I thought you were a doctor," Ken said.

"Professor," the man answered. "Not a college man? No matter. I have a doctorate degree in anthropology. I was tenured at LSU."

Jana sensed the tension building between the two men. "So, do I just open the door, or what?" she asked.

"Oh, no, dear girl," Dr. Dragoon answered. "Subduing the flesh-cage can be unpleasant and I don't let the enquirer watch that. Too unsettling. My men here will take care of that. I have a chair with restraints we'll bring in. First, though, I'm afraid I have to take care of the crass business of seeing the payment you agreed upon."

"Of course," Ken smirked.

"This way," Jana said. She gave Ken a look she hoped he interpreted as *Shut the fuck up* but he didn't acknowledge her. She led the four men back through the library to a small room her father had used for an office. She waved her hand at items piled on her father's desk. The professor and his assistants eyed the offerings.

Dragoon lifted one of two wine bottles and looked at the label, his face beaming. "You really did have the 2005s Philippe Leclerc Cazetiers," he said. "Do you have more?"

"Hey, this is what you asked for," Ken said.

"You need to shut your mouth, nigga," one of Dr. Dragoon's men said. He held Jana's grandfather's World War II Colt .45 in his left hand, his right hand resting on the butt of the cold black Glock in his hip holster. Jana wondered if this man was Andrew or James. Ken gave the man a disgusted look, but didn't speak again.

"It looks like everything is here," Dr. Dragoon said, his eyes fixed on the label of a caviar can, his attitude saying he was pretending not to have noticed the words passed between the other men. "Andrew, James, please take the payment to the helicopter and bring in the equipment. Jana, love, can we use this room for the reading?"

She nodded. "Yes."

"Excellent. Now then, while my men get things arranged and bring in your father, perhaps you would be so kind as to offer me a cool drink?"

Jana led the way to the kitchen and poured the professor a glass of lemonade. She looked at Ken and he nodded, so she poured two more glasses and the three sat down at a table.

"How did you figure out you could do this?" Jana asked.

"It was quite simple," the professor said. "By observing them, you can see immediately that the zombies retain something of what they knew in life. They are still gathering at shopping malls, grocery stores, movie theaters and other places where humans socialized. When they turn, if offered a choice between a loved one and a stranger, the zombie will invariably go for the person they recognize.

"With that in mind, I subdued one of my students who had the unfortunate luck of waking up dead. I strapped her into a chair so that she couldn't eat me, and, well … probed her mentally."

"Like a psychic?"

"Yes. Exactly. I've always had the gift, though I seldom let anyone know about it before. Now, however," he paused and smiled. "A psychic professor is hardly the strangest thing even amongst the limited menagerie under your own roof at the present time."

"True," Jana agreed.

"How will we know what you say is real?" Ken demanded.

"Oh, you'll know, my good man. You'll see evidence."

The professor told them two stories about past experiences communicating with the dead and was beginning a third when one of his wranglers entered the kitchen and said they were ready for him.

"Thank you, James," he said, then turned to Jana. "If you'll pardon me for a few minutes, I will go into the room and compose myself and establish a connection with your father. Once that's done, James here will bring you in. Remember, you must only speak to me. I will relay any questions you have to your father. Understand?"

Jana nodded, then watched the thin man leave with his hulking assistant. Ken broke her reverie.

"This is such fucking bullshit," he said. "I don't care if you give him the wine and fish eggs, but do you have to give up guns and ammunition for this? We could use those."

"We still have plenty of weapons," Jana reminded.

"He asked for more wine. I tell you, he's going to turn those thugs – and that fucking Gatlin gun – loose on us. He's not leaving here content with two bottles of that fancy-ass wine."

"Sometimes, Ken, I'm surprised you have enough trust to get naked with me," Jana said. "Is that why you always have to be on top, the dominant position? Because you're afraid I'll turn on you if I'm on top?"

"I'm a realist." He ignored her questions about their lovemaking. "Greed is the strongest impulse in human nature."

"He's right," James said from the doorway. Jana turned to face the wooden-faced black man who still wore his sunglasses in the house. "About the greed part. But we don't plan on killing you, so long as you don't fuck with us. It's bad for business. Dragoon helps the little lady here, she gets on the CB and tells somebody else, and that person calls on us for help. Dead people and zombies don't use the CB, my man."

Jana sensed Ken about to make some retort. She cut him off. "Can we go in now?"

"Yeah, you can go in," the visitor said.

Jana hurried toward her dead father's office. The door was open, and the smell hit her long before she crossed the threshold. James and Ken were behind her, so there was no turning back. Jana breathed through her mouth and forged ahead, but had to stop in the doorway when her eyes found her father strapped into a tall wooden chair.

His flesh had turned an ashy gray color and was hanging on his frame in most places. In others the meat had erupted and was writhing with maggots. The flesh around his eyes and mouth was loose; Jana could see that he'd lost several teeth and that his gums had receded. A heavy, thick leather strap was fastened over his chest, keeping him in the chair. Two smaller straps pinned his biceps to the back of the chair; his hands rested on the chair's arms as if he'd chosen to sit there and relax for a moment. His eyes were cloudy but focused on the angular professor sitting across from him.

"Dr. Dragoon will ask him yes or no questions," James explained, motioning Jana and Ken into the room to a position out of the zombie's sightline. Andrew remained standing next to the chair the professor sat in. "For yes, the zom—your father will raise his right arm. For no, his left."

*Daddy should be sitting where Dr. Dragoon is. It's his desk.* Jana shook the thought away. It didn't matter.

Dr. Dragoon and his subject stared at one another and it was hard to tell who was hungrier for whom. There was no sound, only the smell of rot and death. Then the professor broke the silence. "I would communicate with the spirit of Alexander Wikel. I know you are trapped in this rotting carcass. While we share this psychic bond I give you the power to partially control your former body. Do you hear and understand me?"

Jana felt her own eyes widen as the thing that used to read her bedtime stories and tuck her in at night suddenly lifted its right arm several inches. "Oh my God," she whispered. Ken had no comment.

"Alexander Wikel, do you know that your daughter is here with us?"

Again, the reanimated corpse raised its right hand.

"Do you remember loving your daughter?"

Jana watched her father answer positively.

"Do you still love your daughter?"

Yes.

"Do you wish to hurt your daughter?"

For the first time, the left hand lifted a few inches into the air. A tear slid down Jana's face.

"Alexander Wikel, we have the power to set your soul free of the rotting cage that holds you here. Do you understand what I mean?"

Yes.

"Is it your desire that we release you from this hell on earth?"

Yes.

"No," Jana whispered.

"Ask him something only he would know," Ken urged softly.

Jana considered it, wondering if it would be a breach of trust to test Dr. Dragoon in such a way.

"They forget a lot of stuff," James said.

"Ask him if he remembers giving me a paint pony for my twelfth birthday," Jana said. *It was a bay. He'll know it was a bay pony.*

"Alexander Wikel," Dr. Dragoon intoned. "Your daughter asks if you recall giving her a pony on her twelfth birthday. Do you remember that?"

No.

"Told you," James said. "It's like Alzheimer's."

"Yes and no questions are so limiting," Jana said, more to herself. Then, louder, "Is there anything he wants to say to me before … before he's … released?"

"Alexander Wikel, is there anything you wish to say to your daughter before we release you?"

Yes.

"Is it an apology for something you did when you were alive?"

No.

"Is it an apology for something you didn't do?"

"A lot of them say yes to this one," James said.

No.

"Is it simply that you love her and miss her?"

Yes.

Jana couldn't stop the sob that burst from her throat. She turned and buried her face in Ken's chest and felt his huge, strong, loving hands on her back, caressing and comforting her. "I'm sorry," she cried into his chambray shirt.

"Alexander Wikel, my assistant will now release you. May you find peace," Dr. Dragoon said.

Jana started to raise her head, believing she should bear witness, but Ken's heavy hand kept her face pressed against his chest. There was a shot, then a long moment of thick silence. Ken's hand slipped away and Jana turned to look at her father.

He was truly dead now. There was a small hole in his forehead and a splattering of thick red and gray goo on the floor behind the chair. Andrew holstered his pistol.

"Our work here is done," Dr. Dragoon said, rising from his chair. "James and Andrew will take the body out of the chair, but I'm afraid it's up to you to dispose of it."

"Is he ... Did he find peace?" Jana asked.

"I think so," the professor answered.

Jana nodded. "Thank you," she said.

"Let's go have another glass of lemonade. Shall we?"

"Okay," Jana agreed. She slipped out of Ken's arms and turned toward the door. That's when she saw Tom standing in the doorway. He had his 30.06 rifle to his shoulder. A hard hand shoved Jana out of the way and as she was falling to the floor she saw Ken drawing his pistol with his other hand.

Tom's rifle fired first, then Ken's pistol. James and Andrew both fell to the floor. Andrew's feet twitched on the carpet. Ken stepped closer, pointed his gun at the other man's head, and said, "Now you shut *your* mouth, nigga." His gun exploded and Andrew was still.

Outside, another rifle sounded. Once, then twice.

"That would be Lamar," Ken said.

There was a moment of silence, then Dr. Dragoon asked softly, "Why?"

"You're a sham, you slick fuck," Ken said.

"Ken, what the hell are you doing?" Jana screamed. She got up and charged the big man, her fists clenched, ready to pound the chest she had been crying on only moments ago. He caught her with one strong arm and held her close.

"It's an old trick, baby," Ken said. "This man kept your attention on what he was doing with your dad while his goon manipulated the controls that made the body answer."

"That's not true," Jana argued. "You're just saying – "

"I'll show you," Ken said. He released Jana, but looked to Tom. "Keep your gun on him. Kill him if he moves."

"Gladly," Tom answered. His watery eyes were emotionless. "Preying on the hopeful. Despicable."

Ken went to the chair where Alexander Wikel's dead body sat. He loosened the leather cuffs holding the corpse's right arm to the back of the chair and pulled the arm free. A red-sheathed electrical wire was threaded through a hole in the back of the cuff and fastened to the body's arm. Ken pulled the wire out to reveal that it was attached to a long needle that had been inserted into the arm.

Dr. Dragoon remained silent.

"Now, watch this," Ken said. He moved to the body of Andrew, pushed the corpse over with his boot, then took a small black item from Andrew's hand. "I push this button on the left and ..." He pushed the button and Alexander Wikel's left arm raised several inches off the chair's armrest.

"You ... you're a liar," Jana said, staring at the man in the gray suit. He gave a half-smile and shrugged his shoulders. "And you killed him. You bastard!" Jana reached for the gun strapped to her own waist.

"Wait," Ken said, his voice sharp and commanding. "We can do better than that. Come in here, Lamar."

Jana turned to see Lamar Kennedy enter the room, his own high-powered rife with its assassin scope held loosely in his hands. He wasn't as big as Ken, but his skin was darker, making his eyes and teeth seem to glow in his head.

"The chopper's ours?" Ken asked.

"Yup. Shot the gunner first. His head fuckin' exploded, G. The pilot tried to get the bird started, but I capped him through the side window. We got us a fuckin' Blackhawk, baby!"

"Get some rope and tie this man's hands," Ken said. "I think he wants to play some tennis."

"Lance will enjoy the company," Tom drawled.

"How could you?" Jana asked, coming to stand in front of the professor. "How could you take advantage of people like that?"

"Wake up, sweetie," Dr. Dragoon said. "People have always been willing to pay shamans to tell them what they want to hear. Only the circumstances and technology have changed. You heard what you wanted."

"I wanted the truth."

"I call bullshit, little missy." His voice was little more than a hiss now. "You wanted him to say he was sorry for touching you? For not touching you? For ignoring your mother, forgetting your birthday or screwing his secretary? No. You wanted to hear that your daddy has always loved you and that he wanted a bullet in the head so you wouldn't feel guilty about shooting him. I gave you all of that. And you, you gave me this." He motioned to his dead associates.

"Fuck you." Jana turned to Ken. "I'll be waiting at the tennis court."

She passed Tom in the library as he took a length of rope to Ken. Jana left the house, returning to the sweltering heat of late morning. She trudged across the yard, ignoring the helicopter, but listening to the regular gurgle of the swimming pool pump. *No electricity for air conditioning, but we keep the pool pump going.* Down a grassy incline on the far end of the pool was the tennis court with its tall fence and red clay floor.

Locked inside the court was Lance Langam. Once almost corpulent, he was now just a corpse. The two female zombies who shared his pen had eaten most of his soft belly and part of his arms before he reanimated. One of the female zombies noticed Jana and moaned excitedly as she shuffled toward the fence.

*I can't believe Lance even thought about fucking these things.*

Granted, the young zombie in the black leather miniskirt hadn't been as decayed at the time, but still.

"Lead them away from the gate!" It was Ken's voice. Jana looked toward the top of the rise and saw her man – Daddy never would have approved of her loving a black man – as he led Dr. Dragoon toward the tennis court. The professor's hands were tied behind his back and Ken held the other end of the rope. Both Tom and Lamar flanked the professor, their pistols drawn.

Jana strolled leisurely toward the far end of the tennis court. All three zombies had come to the fence to moan and reach for her now and they followed her as she walked. She could hear the professor begging his captors.

"I'll give you anything," Dr. Dragoon promised. "I have unbelievable wealth at my own compound. Alcohol, drugs, books, gasoline. You name your desire and I can grant it."

"We desire that you shut the fuck up, G," Lamar laughed.

Ken dug a set of keys from his pocket and tossed them to Tom, who unlocked the gate of the tennis court. "Let's see you form that psychic connection with these zombies," Ken said. "The man's name is Lance. We don't know his lady friends."

"I'm begging you, sir," Dr. Dragoon said. "Don't do this."

"Push him in there!" Jana screamed.

Ken shoved the man through the open gate and Tom slammed it shut and snapped the heavy padlock. The professor, his hands still tied behind him, continued to plead his case. Jana began the stroll back toward her companions, her undead audience following her until they realized there was meat in the pen with them.

Dr. Dragoon avoided the zombies for almost an hour, but eventually the heat and constant running wore him out and he collapsed. Jana hoped he was still conscious when they bit into him.

"I think we've earned a swim," Ken said.

"I think so," Jana agreed. Later, as she floated on an air mattress beside Ken, she said, "I suppose you're going to say I told you so at some point."

"About what?"

"Human nature. Everyone's greedy. Maybe Dragoon wasn't going to kill us all like you said, but he was a sham. He was robbing us."

"I suppose I could say it," Ken said. "But hell, thanks to you bringing him here, we got us a mighty fine piece of transportation. We'll be able to scavenge a lot further now, bring in more food from further away, and that Gatlin gun ..." He whistled. "That'll make the morning work go a lot faster."

"You know how to fly that thing?" Jana asked.

"Not yet, but I'll learn. First, though, I think we should go inside. You had some other delusion about me needing to be in control and I think we can fix that."

"Bullshit, man!" Lamar yelled from his own air mattress. "G, we're taking that chopper out and finding me my own woman as soon as one of us can fly it. Shit!"

"The world has ended," Tom mused. "We're feeding people to zombies, have no idea if civilization will ever be reestablished, and all you people can think about is sex. Makes me glad my pecker hasn't been hard in ten years."

# ONE NIGHT IN BENEVOLENCE

Drew Parker wheeled his small blue pickup into the driveway of the little white house and killed the engine before making himself look at the dwelling he hadn't faced in over twenty-five years. His hands gripped the steering wheel, squeezing and turning, his eyes fixed on the bluish letters tattooed on the backs of his left fingers. They spelled his name. He'd learned to do the crude tattooing in prison. Everyone in prison found some way to kill time. Finally, he looked at the house.

It seemed so much smaller than he'd remembered. The paint was peeling from the siding and the screen door hung crookedly from a broken hinge. The porch swing hadn't been painted in years; it was weathered and faded, hanging on a rusty chain. Behind a drawn shade a light burned with an amber glow that should have been welcoming.

"He's dead," Drew muttered. "He isn't here anymore."

Then the front door of the house opened and a thin, gray-haired woman stepped onto the porch. The wear on her face added too many years to the sixty-one she'd actually lived, but her eyes lit when she saw her son in the driveway, and Drew couldn't suppress his own smile as he opened the truck door and went to hug his mother.

"Oh Drew, it's been too long," she said.

Drew was keenly aware of how tiny she felt in his embrace and how frail her arms seemed to be as they pressed him tighter to her.

*Osteoporosis. I know she used to be bigger.*

"Hi, Mom," he said. "Are you sure about this? It seems kind of crazy."

"Maybe it just took a crazy scheme to get you to come home," she said, letting go of him and stepping back. Her eyes were shimmering with unspent tears.

Drew inhaled sharply and bit back his initial response. "Maybe," he said.

"I made tea," she said. "Let's have a glass while we wait for the moon to come up."

Drew followed her inside. The smell was like a punch in the face. Not a bad smell. It was a mixture of many, many meals, pine cleaners, fresh cookies, and memories he didn't want to face. The furniture was different than it had been when he'd left, but the pieces were similar and arranged just as they'd been so long ago. His mother led him through the living room to the kitchen, where a glass pitcher of iced tea waited with lemon slices floating in it.

"My God," Drew said. "Is that the same refrigerator?"

"Oh, yes," she admitted. "It never quit working, so we never replaced it."

For a moment Drew saw his overweight father in his gray uniform pants and stained white undershirt leaning into the refrigerator for another brown bottle of beer. He shook his head and the image broke apart. His mother was holding a glass of tea toward him. Drew took it and sat down with her.

"You should have come to the funeral," she said.

"No." Drew sipped his tea.

"He was your father."

"Yeah. That's why he kept telling me he knew you were a whore because he never would have fathered a piece of shit like me."

"Drew!" The light in her eyes faded for a moment and she looked even older as the shadow of forty-some years of marital oppression passed over her face.

"I'm sorry, Mom," Drew said.

"Those were just words," she said. "He didn't mean them."

Drew grunted and sipped tea.

"I heard from your Aunty Ruby the other day," his mom said. She launched into a story about her sister-in-law's ailments.

*Look at her. She's almost happy, but she still denies she married a monster. I haven't seen her more than twice in the twenty-five years since I went to prison and she talks like it's been a week. But then, how long was she in her own hell? She developed mechanisms to deal with it*

Drew realized his thoughts were scattered. The idea of being back in his childhood home in the small eastern Oklahoma town of Benevolence was getting to him. He stared at a window over the kitchen sink, watching the evening darken between his old home and the empty Astor house next door as his mom talked and his mind moved backward in time.

\* \* \*

25

Drew had been seven years old when his father had caught him looking at his *Playboy* collection. "You've been snooping through my private shit again, boy," the man roared as he unfastened his belt.

"No, Dad, no," Drew begged. "Please, not the belt."

"You gotta learn to respect my fuckin' privacy, you little shit. Them books was in my private dresser and you been snooping through there. Yer lucky I caught you before your mother saw you lookin' at them dirty books."

"You look at them," Drew said.

Then the belt, curses, and beer-flavored spittle were flying. There was nothing Drew could do but cower beside his parents' bed, keeping his arms over his head as his father lashed him with the thick leather belt and assurances that he was nothing now, was never anything but a fucking mistake and would never amount to shit.

*Just words.*

His mother always treated the bruises and lashes with love, promising that the curses and insults were just words. "Words can't hurt you," she promised, her own arms purple and yellow as testament to what happened when dinner was late. "They can't hurt you if he doesn't mean them, and he doesn't."

*Bullshit.*

The day after that whipping, Drew recalled, the old man came home from work with a tiny black-and-brown puppy. His father never apologized for the beating. He just put the dog in Drew's trembling hands and said, "Maybe this'll keep you outta trouble."

And he had, mostly. Drew named the dog Bilbo, after the little guy with the hairy feet in a cartoon movie he'd seen on TV. The Bilbo in that story helped kill a dragon. Drew's Bilbo helped keep the boy from getting killed.

* * *

"I think it's dark enough."

"What?" Drew asked, pulled back to the present.

"It's dark enough," his mother repeated.

"Oh." Drew put his empty glass on the table. He couldn't remember finishing the drink. "It's so weird to be back here."

"I'm glad you came, Drew." She reached out and gripped his hand. He could feel the bones beneath the thin flesh of her fingers.

He nodded. "Me, too. Now, let's do this thing."

She laughed, a musical, tinkling laugh he suddenly realized he'd missed. "Will you get the bucket?" She pointed to a galvanized metal pail near the back door of the house. It was filled with white bulbs. "The shovel is already in the back yard."

Drew lifted the bucket and opened the door. The boards of the back porch groaned under his weight and the roof sagged so low it almost brushed his head as he moved beneath it. "You should have someone tear this porch down and rebuild it," he said.

"Is that an offer?"

Drew snorted. "My carpentry skills haven't improved," he said.

She laughed. "I remember that doghouse you built."

"Yeah." Drew smiled at the thought of the leaky, crooked structure. *Twice now I've thought of Bilbo.* He eyes moved across the darkened yard to the chain link fence at the back, just left of the furthest post in the right-hand corner. *He's buried right there.*

"Watch your step."

The warning was too late. Drew's foot caught on the edge of a cement curb that marked off a section of the back yard and he fell to his knees, dropping the pail to catch himself with his hands. Tulip bulbs spilled all around him.

The previous owners had used the marked-off area as a flowerbed. His mother had always wanted flowers there, Drew knew, but the only thing that had been planted within the rectangle during his family's ownership of the home was the body of a murdered dog.

Drew sat down and rubbed his ankle, looking at the exposed section of curb that had tripped him. *Fucking hole is still here.* He remembered having to be careful mowing the low spot so the mower blade wouldn't hit the concrete. He'd broken a blade on the four-inch-wide curb when he was ten years old.

\* \* \*

The blade struck the concrete with an incredible bang. Sparks flew from the grass chute of the Lawnboy mower and the engine died.

"Goddammit boy!" his father roared. Before Drew could look up, something slammed into his head. He crumpled to the ground, stars popping before his eyes, the nearly full beer bottle glugging into his lap. "You broke that fuckin' blade off, dinnitya? Fucker. Worthless fuck."

Drew's vision cleared in time for him to see his father's white undershirt going through the back door of the house. The door slammed and a few moments later the obese man reappeared at the kitchen window, a fresh brown beer bottle at his lips.

Bilbo came to Drew's side. The cocker spaniel-mix dog sniffed his face, then licked a single tear from Drew's cheek, his tail wagging enthusiastically.

Later, Drew's mother had apologized. "He doesn't mean it, honey," she soothed. "Your dad has a lot on his mind. Things aren't going good at the refinery. Don't you pay any attention to what he says when he's been drinking. They're just words. He doesn't mean them. He loves you."

She'd been wearing long-sleeved shirts all the time, even in the sticky hot summers by then because of the knowing, sad looks offered by people who saw her in the grocery store, post office and welfare office.

"He doesn't mean those hurtful things," she lied.

*Just words.*

\* \* \*

"Are you okay?"

"Yes," Drew answered. His mother was on her knees beside him. All the white tulip bulbs were back in the bucket.

*When did she pick those up?*

"I didn't know how much it would get to me, being back here," Drew said. "I'm sorry, Mom, but I've got to say I'm glad the old man is dead. God, I hated him."

"Those are only words, Drew, and I know you don't mean them."

Drew shook his head. "You always say that, Mom. Don't any words mean anything? If I tell you I love you, does that mean anything?"

"Of course it does," she answered, smiling brightly. "Good words always have meaning."

"But bad ones don't?"

"No."

Drew started to protest, then let it go. In his job as a social worker, helping children in broken homes, he'd seen the same denial mechanism at play many times. The kids pretended everything was fine. Their mothers fooled themselves into believing the abusive man would come around, or that he really wasn't so bad ... that he didn't really mean it. Drew sighed. *At least Mom outlived the bastard and can be happy for the years she has left.*

"So, who told you these tulips would grow better if you planted them in moonlight?" he asked.

"It was Ruby. She's always had a green thumb. Your aunt could plant a tin can and grow a Cadillac. One time she ..."

The story continued, but Drew tuned it out. He got to his feet and sank the tip of the spade into the ground and turned over a blade of dark, moist, loamy earth. The smell reminded him of digging worms for fishing trips to the Illinois River with his friends. *And Bilbo.* He continued to dig, moving around the edge of the rectangular curb as his mother explained how his aunt had grown prize-winning flowers and vegetables.

Suddenly the shovel hit something solid.

"What was that?" his mother asked.

Drew stared at the ground where he'd been digging. The moonlight was pale and cast dark shadows, but his position relative to the back fence told Drew where he was. *I'm standing right over Bilbo's grave.*

\* \* \*

At the age of sixteen, Drew had been in a car with three friends from Benevolence High School. Randy, the owner of the car, went into a Circle K store and a few minutes later came running out. He jumped into the car, a rusted Ford Maverick, tossed a carton of Marlboro cigarettes into Drew's lap and burned rubber out of the parking lot. The police were behind them before they were a mile from the store.

Randy went to jail. Drew and the other two boys had to wait in the police station until their parents arrived. Drew remembered wishing they would put him in a cell instead of turning him over to his father. The beating had been brutal.

"I gotta take off work to get you out of jail! Yer fucking with my fucking job now, you worthless turd." No belt this time. Due to his size, Drew had graduated to the world his mother knew so well – punishment by fist.

He never returned to school after that. At first he'd been too ashamed to go back because of the black eyes and swollen lip. By the time the swelling and discoloration had left his face, he just didn't care. He took a full-time bag-boy job at Wilson's Grocery and began saving money to move out of his father's house.

His time off was spent talking with Bilbo about how much better it would be when they got away.

"Them's just bullshit words," his father said when he overheard part of the conversation one day. "You got a job now, you can start payin' me some fuckin' rent for living in my goddamn house."

So it went for well over a year. Then, a week before Drew's eighteenth birthday, his father ran over his dog in the driveway. Drew had been outside, working on his Oldsmobile by flashlight, putting in a new thermostat and talking to Bilbo. The dog's black hair was beginning to turn gray around his eyes by that time and he was no longer as active as he'd once been. Drew's father had gone to a convenience store for more beer, but had already had a few. When he returned home he didn't see the arthritic dog sleeping in the driveway, or so he said.

Bilbo's death hadn't been quick or painless. The pickup truck crushed his hips. Bilbo yelped, caught as he tried to get away from the tire. He continued to cry in loud, sharp, pitiful barks for several minutes.

Drew's father got out of the truck, his six-pack of Budweiser in one hand, his other hand pulling his sweat pants out of his crotch. He looked from the dog to Drew, who was crouching beside Bilbo, trying to comfort him.

"Fucker was in the way."

"You killed him," Drew said without looking up. "You fucking bastard."

His father's fist caught him on the temple and sent him sprawling across the driveway. When Drew was able to sit up and shake the blackness from his vision, his father was gone. But the man came back around the front of the house a moment later with his nickel-plated .22 caliber pistol in his hand.

"No!" Drew screamed.

His father aimed the gun and shot at Bilbo, aiming for his head. But he was too drunk. The first bullet missed completely. The second caught the dog in the throat. Bilbo yelped again, but it was a raspy sound that whistled through the bloody hole in his throat. The third bullet penetrated his skull and silenced him.

"He was gonna die anyway. That just made it quicker. Ended his pain. And shut him up." The old man staggered back a step, then turned around and left the dead dog and the crying young man alone in the driveway.

* * *

32

"It looks like a wooden box."

"Huh?" Drew shook his head. His hands were empty. He blinked and looked around for his mother. He found her crouched over a hole in the flowerbed. She looked up at him and the moonlight reflected in her eyes.

"Drew, are you okay?"

"Yeah. I'm okay. It's just ... you know. So many memories. I really didn't expect this."

"This is a wooden box," his mother said, looking back toward the hole.

Drew nodded. "I know. Did you dig all that out?" He looked with amazement at the pile of dirt piled around the hole. "You shouldn't be doing that."

"Oh, nonsense. I'm stronger than you think. But you look pale. Sit down for a minute while I go get a flashlight."

Her knees popped and crackled as she stood up. Drew watched her walk back toward the house, then he turned to the hole and dropped down beside it.

"Bilbo," he whispered. "The only good thing about my whole rotten childhood is right here."

Only about nine inches of the wooden box was visible. *I thought I buried him at least three feet deep.* Another trick of youth, like believing his childhood home was bigger than it was. The top of the box wasn't more than five inches beneath the surface of the earth. Drew reached out with a trembling hand and touched the cool pine wood.

\* \* \*

His father's alcoholism had finally cost him his job at the refinery. At the age of eighteen, Drew took a job with one of the companies that rented out canoes to city people who wanted to ride down the river. The pay was low, but better than he'd had at the grocery store. His small checks kept the family from losing the house and electricity, though they could no longer afford to have a telephone or cable television.

After a particularly hard day at work, Drew came home to find his father sitting in his favorite recliner, drinking from a Jack Daniels bottle. "I don't earn the money so you can drink it all," he snapped. "Mom wants the phone turned back on."

His father exploded out of his worn recliner. His hard fists pounded Drew's face and torso as he cursed him. "You think yer better'n me now? You shit! You fuckin' *shit!* I never wanted you." Drew was huddled on the floor, blood running from his nose and mouth, pain shooting through his chest. His father kicked him before continuing. "I never wanted you. Your mother was just too stupid. Too stupid to take the fuckin' pill."

Then it was over and the older man staggered off toward his bedroom. A moment later, Drew felt another touch on his face. He flinched before opening his eyes to find his mother hovering over him. She pressed a cold washcloth to his cheek, dabbing at the blood.

"He doesn't mean it," she said.

"Only words," Drew added before she could. Blood sprayed from his busted lips as he spoke.

"They can't hurt you if he doesn't mean them," she said.

That was the first time he'd realized she looked older than a woman of her age should look. She smiled at him, but it was the forced smile of a frightened creature held in a cage.

"Why do you let him treat you this way?"

"He doesn't mean it. He's a good man, Drew. He really is."

Drew pushed himself away from her and went to his room. Later that night, he showered and packed a suitcase. The next day he went to work and emptied the cash register drawer into a paper sack. A customer saw him and tried to stop him as he left the boat rental office. Drew broke the man's jaw with a canoe oar. Other customers screamed. The store owner picked up the phone and Drew ran.

He didn't make it out of the county before the police caught him. He was charged with robbery, aggravated assault and evading arrest. Drew was convicted on all counts. After eighteen months he was released, but jailed again six weeks later for home invasion.

\* \* \*

"That's all over now," he muttered. "It was a long time ago. I've changed. I've got my own place now. And a good job working with troubled kids so they don't end up like I was." The sob came unexpectedly, bursting through his throat from deep in his chest. Drew slumped over the hole and let tears fall into the grave. "I miss talking to you, buddy," he said.

"Drew?"

He quickly wiped at his face and sat up before turning to face his mother. She shone a flashlight in his general direction.

"Are you alright?"

He nodded. "I'm fine. Just remembering Bilbo. This is where I buried him."

"It is? I thought you buried him by the river."

"No. I was afraid some city slicker would dig him up by accident." He paused. "But instead, we did it."

"You could take him with you," she said.

"What?"

"Take him with you. Rebury him at your house."

Drew looked back at the hole. "I don't know."

"I know he meant a lot to you, Drew. You should have him where you can talk to him. He can still hear you, you know."

"Doggy heaven?"

"That's right," she said.

He shook his head. His right eye burned. "I got dirt in my eye," he said. "I'm gonna run inside and rinse it out."

He got to his feet and hurried past his mother before she could get a better look at the mud and tears on his face. Back in the house, he found the bathroom – again, it seemed incredibly tiny compared to his memory of it – and washed his face, dabbing handfuls of water onto his open eye until it stopped burning. He turned off the faucet and stared at his wet reflection.

"You've got to get hold of yourself, dumbass," he said. "You're here to help your mother plant flowers. That's it. Do it and get away. Next time it'll be easier. It'll be easier every time I come back."

He dried his face and his eyes came to rest on the toilet. The lid was covered in a fuzzy pink cover that looked new. He knew his father had died sitting on that toilet. *Elvis died on his throne, too.* Duane Parker had been straining to take a shit and stroked out. Drew found that to be a fitting end for the man. He hung up the towel and left the bathroom.

His mother was kneeling beside the hole again and the pile of dirt around her was even higher. Drew shook his head, marveling at her strength and determination. She heard him approaching and turned to look at him. He saw she was shining her flashlight into the grave.

"There's something written on the top of this box," she said.

Drew froze. He remembered going to the railroad yard the day after Bilbo died. There were always wooden boxes around there. He'd found one and brought it home, where he wrapped the dog's body in gunny sacks before laying it in the box and nailing down the lid.

*And ...*

Something else.

He watched his mom return her attention to the hole. She reached in and lifted out a handful of dark dirt. "It looks like it's burned into the wood. You did have that woodburning kit. I remember you writing on scrap wood all the time with that."

"Mom ..."

"Bilbo, may you return from the dead to destroy the soul of anyone who disturbs you." She turned to look at Drew, a small smile stretching the wrinkles over her upper lip. "Only a boy could believe in curses," she said. "They're – "

"Only words," Drew finished. "They can't hurt anybody unless you mean them." He remembered worrying that his father would disturb the dog's grave. "Unless you mean them," he repeated.

Far away, a dog snarled. Drew looked up, but couldn't determine the direction of the sound.

Steven E. Wedel

"That's just one of those pit bulls those Mexican boys down the street have," his mother said.

"Are you sure?"

"Of course. Help me up. My knees aren't what they used to be."

"I could have told you that," Drew said. He extended a hand to his mother and she put her own wrinkled hand into it.

Then the dog growled again.

*May you return from the dead ...*

Drew's mouth suddenly felt very dry. The snarl came again, low and menacing, turning into a growl. But now Drew could determine the location. The sound was coming from behind him. He saw that his mother had already found the source. Her hand slipped out of his as Drew turned to look behind him.

For the briefest moment he saw Bilbo running at them. The dog's body was ghostly, shimmering, his tail down, his black lips pulled back to show his teeth. His tan feet were not touching the ground as he ran full speed. Bilbo's eyes were brown fire, filled with hate and rage. The dog lunged forward.

"No!" Drew screamed as the vaporous shape flew at his mother. He blocked the dog's path, but the ethereal form passed through him. A blazing lance of pain shot through his body and he stumbled forward, dropping to the ground and burying his face in the freshly turned soil. He heard his mother scream and he pushed himself up, shaking his head to clear the dirt from his eyes.

*May you return from the dead to destroy the soul of anyone who disturbs you.*

The ghostly image of Bilbo was nowhere to be seen. Drew found his mother laying on the ground, moaning and rocking back and forth. He smelled burned meat as he reached for her. Then he saw a glow coming from the open grave.

The makeshift coffin exploded, sending splinters of wood flying in all directions. Drew felt the shards embedding themselves in his face and arms as he tried to shield himself. Then he heard the dog growling again. He lowered his arms and saw Bilbo standing before him.

The dog was bigger than he should have been. Unlike Drew's childhood home, or even his mother, which seemed so much smaller upon his return, the dog that had been no taller than two feet in life had grown massive in his memory. The beast glowed as if with grave gases. Rancid slobber fell from his bared fangs.

"Bilbo …?" Drew asked, but the dog ignored him, focusing instead on the woman who had unearthed his coffin.

Drew watched as his mother looked up and saw the dog. She screamed. He screamed, too, and threw himself at the dog. But he bounced off the strange body of the animal, the air suddenly knocked from his lungs. The dog lunged forward. Drew heard his mother's screaming rise in pitch, then it came to a sudden stop.

"She didn't mean to," Drew sobbed. "You were supposed to kill the old man."

Drew opened his eyes. His head was in the hole his mother had dug. The flashlight lay on top of the intact lid of his dog's coffin, the beam of light illuminating the words burned into the old wood.

*Everyone in abusive situations develops coping mechanisms …*

Drew forced himself to his hands and knees and turned to find his mother. The phantom dog was gone. His mother's body lay twisted on the ground, her head misshapen like a dropped jack-o-lantern. The long-handled shovel lay beside her. The backside of the shovel blade was covered in dark blood and sticky tufts of gray hair.

"Mom ... I'm sorry. I didn't mean it."

# DEAD BETTY

Professor Anthony Daniels looked at the naked young man in the wooden chair and thought about how college students will do just about anything for money. The kid, Brandon Plummer, already had an erection. But, that was good, Anthony thought. *Get it over quick.*

The chair Plummer sat in had a rubber mat covering the back and seat. The armrests and front legs were also wrapped in rubber. Plummer's forearms and calves were fastened to the chair with Velcro straps. A blue plastic shield was fixed in place just inches in front of Plummer's face to protect his identity and that of the young woman kneeling between his knees.

"You know what to do?" Anthony asked. "I mean, you know how?"

The girl, Stephanie Jackson, nodded. Her mousy brown hair was loose and fell over the shoulders of her blue sweater. She was a rather plain-looking creature, Anthony thought. But, with this kind of experiment, that was to be expected. She was nervous, but that was okay. Like

Plummer, she had been instructed not to speak during the experiment.

"You may begin," Anthony said.

The girl took Plummer's stiff penis in her right hand and leaned over his lap. She wrapped her lips around him and slid down to her fist, then back up, then down again. Plummer groaned. Anthony saw the boy's fingers clinch on the armrests. The needles inserted into the fingers of his left hand remained in place. Electrical wires covered in red plastic sheathing ran from Plummer's fingers to a Mason jar filled with a milky white substance – fat from a black bear. The sheathing of the wires was cut away inside the jar and the individual copper wires spread out like roots through the lard.

Anthony's left index finger caressed a red button that would send a jolt of electricity through the white-sheathed wires attached to Plummer's head. Not yet, but soon.

Plummer said he'd received oral sex twice before. He'd had actual intercourse four times. Jackson claimed to have given oral sex on numerous occasions because she refused to "put out" in any other way and "guys expect something." Anthony didn't expect it to take long for Plummer to climax; Jackson obviously really did know what she was doing.

The girl held Plummer's penis and ran her tongue down the underside of the shaft until she had his testicle sack in her mouth. She sucked vigorously while squeezing and pulling his cock. Plummer's buttocks were clenching with each upward pull. If he hadn't been so intent on pushing the red button at the exact moment, Anthony knew he could watch this exhibition for the sheer pleasure of it.

He hoped his own time for such pleasure was not so far away.

The professor sat to the side of the spectacle so he could watch what the girl did while at the same time gauging the boy's face for the right moment to zap him.

Jackson took Plummer's penis in her mouth again and bobbed her head up and down rapidly, her small hands clutching his thighs, her hair bouncing. Plummer's butt rose from the chair.

"Oh God, here I come," he said through a grimace.

Anthony waited a split second, then pushed his button. Plummer shrieked and threw his hips forward. Jackson pulled back, choking from the sudden thrust, and was sprayed in the face with an unwinding spool of Plummer's semen.

The professor saw all this in his periphery vision; the students no longer mattered. His focus was on the bear fat. Sparks flew from the frayed copper wires and suddenly the entire glob of fat was stained a deep reddish-orange. A thin tendril of smoke twisted through the mouth of the jar and dissipated in the room.

"Perfect," Anthony whispered. "Just perfect."

"Gross! Do you have a towel?"

Anthony looked away from the jar. Stephanie Jackson was wiping semen from her left cheek. Her hair was matted with the goo. She wasn't supposed to talk, Anthony thought, unless she wanted the boy to know her identity.

"No, I'm afraid not," Anthony said. "You'll have to go to the restroom across the hall. You can pick up your check in my office tomorrow afternoon."

The girl gave him a disgusted look as she got to her feet and started walking away.

"Hey!" Brandon Plummer called. He was trying to see around the shield in front of his face. "I don't know who you are, but that was great. I'm Brandon Plummer. Call me if you want to go out sometime."

The girl never looked back; the lab door slammed behind her. Anthony pulled the needles from Plummer's fingers, not bothering to be too careful, removed the electrodes from his temples, and sent him on his way.

The professor reverently lifted his Mason jar and peered deeply into its contents. The fat was even swirling -- just a little, but there was definite movement. Anthony gently placed the jar on a lab table equipped with a gas outlet for a Bunsen burner, then went to lock all the doors to the lab.

When he came back, he used a spoon to dip out some fat and pushed it into the bottom of a test tube. He fired up a burner and held the test tube in the flickering blue flame, watching the fat darken in color as it melted to a liquid. He hummed a tuneless little song as he worked.

When the fat was completely liquefied, he put the test tube in a rack and hurried to another table -- a long, stainless steel table split lengthwise down the center with a well beneath. He mashed down on a foot pedal; the table opened and the cadaver housed inside rose to the level of the tabletop.

The cadaver was a fresh one -- a middle-aged female, just delivered to the university the day before. No students had been hacking on this one yet. The woman -- Anthony called her Betty -- appeared to be perfectly normal, other than being dead. She had been the victim of a sudden heart attack.

She was naked, of course, her body wrapped in heavy, transparent plastic. Her stomach and thighs were a little flabby, Anthony thought as he peeled the plastic away. Her pubic hair was thick and curly; her breasts sagged toward her sides. She hadn't been a totally unattractive woman, but she was no aging supermodel, either.

Anthony took the electrodes that an hour ago had been taped to Brandon Plummer's head and attached them to Betty's temples. He smoothed and parted her hair -- black with a few thin streaks of gray -- until he found the tiny hole he'd drilled into her skull earlier in the day. He smiled and returned to his test tube of boiled bear fat.

The professor took a syringe from a drawer, put a needle on it, and drew five CCs of the rusty-looking fluid from the test tube into the syringe. He squirted a small stream into the air to be sure the bubbles were out, although an air bubble would hardly bother Betty.

Anthony chuckled at his own humor. He went back to the cadaver, smoothed the hair back again, and stuck the needle into the brain, measuring carefully to be sure the tip rested in the center of the pineal gland. He injected his serum into the body and pulled the needle out, tossing the syringe onto a side table.

He nearly pranced as he hurried to the box with the red button on it. He pushed the button, sending a high current of electrical power into the cadaver and, he hoped, fusing the bear fat with the pineal gland -- the gland that supposedly housed the soul in living bodies.

Betty's corpse stiffened, much as Plummer's had during his ejaculation. Anthony could smell a faint scent of burning. Betty's hair stood on end, her nipples suddenly erect, her pubic area a wild, spiked bush of bristling hair. Anthony released the button.

Betty jerked to a sitting position. The electrodes pulled away from her head and fell to the floor. She swung her legs over the edge of the table and faced Anthony.

"You're beautiful, my dear," he said, his voice quiet and filled with awe. Despite all the research and theories, he hadn't been sure this experiment would work.

Betty opened her mouth, working her jaw up and down and side to side. Finally, in a harsh, croaking voice, she said, "Fuck me. Fuck me!"

She jumped off the table and rushed at him. Anthony didn't have time to say anything. He simply held out his arms to embrace her. Betty wasn't interested in snuggling. With amazing strength, she tore at the professor's clothes. Suddenly worried, Anthony tried to back away, but the naked cadaver clutched at him, tearing until his clothes were little more than tatters hanging from his body. She grabbed his semi-erect penis in her hand and pulled fiercely on it.

"Stop," Anthony ordered. "Stop it! Now!" He grimaced as she continued pulling as if she'd rip the root of his manhood right out of his body. Still, he felt himself responding.

"Fuck me!" She pushed him to the floor and straddled him, shoving her dry vagina over his penis and forcing him into her. "Fuck me! Fuck me!" she screamed over and over, bouncing on him like a kid on a spring-horse.

Anthony did it. Her dead body was unable to produce any lubricants, making her vagina extremely tight. Within moments, the professor felt himself ready to ejaculate. He clutched at her, pulled her hips tight over his and grunted deeply as he came. His eruption did nothing to satisfy Betty.

The corpse continued riding him, not even seeming to notice that he'd finished. As he felt his own semen finally providing some lubrication, Anthony realized the flaw in his experiment. Betty was unable to think. She was simply responding to the emotional stimuli he had provided – pure lust.

"Oh God, how could I have been so stupid?"

Betty continued pounding him, her face an animal mask of blind passion that could have been lust, could have been hate. Her body did not seem to respond to the intercourse; Anthony was sure she had not climaxed once during the encounter so far. She simply rode him, relentlessly, angrily, driven by the need he'd given her.

His semen hadn't produced enough moisture in the vaginal cavity to allow him to slip out. He was trapped inside her. Soon, Anthony felt himself chafing. He began to struggle.

Betty was strong, but Anthony managed to push her up just enough to pull his limp, raw cock out of her. Her crotch pounded down on him again, pinning a testicle between her body and his and sending a shooting, sickening pain through his gut. He tried to double over but couldn't.

Apparently, Betty did retain some reasoning power. Her chant of "Fuck me! Fuck me!" suddenly changed. She grabbed Anthony by the head and threw her body forward. "Eat me! Eat me!" she shrieked. "Lick my cunt!"

Anthony gagged on the dry taste of dead flesh and the salty thickness of his own semen dripping from the woman's body. Now, instead of banging up and down on him, Betty used a grinding, rotating motion to force herself over his mouth. Anthony squeezed his eyes closed and began licking her as furiously as he could, forcing all the saliva he could muster into her crotch. Finally, she became wet. He grabbed her butt and pushed her forward while he scooted from under her. His final mistake was pausing to gape at the thing rushing to tackle him.

Betty's face was covered in blisters and sagging around the eye sockets. Her eyes were sizzling and popping as they slowly melted and dripped down her face. The flesh on the arms reaching for the professor was loose and feverish.

"She's burning up from the inside," Anthony whispered. Then Betty had him, her burning arms encircling him, her weight dragging him to the floor.

This time she covered him in a sixty-nine position, popping his floppy penis into her burning mouth and sucking like a devil. The intense heat sparked a return to life within him and Anthony felt himself hardening again as Betty pushed her decaying pussy back toward his mouth. The skin of her thighs sloughed away where she made contact with his chest and shoulders. The muscles coated in congealed blood beneath the skin were like napalm pressing against Anthony.

"How long until she burns up?" he moaned as the fried, spiked pubic hair slammed into his face again. She was wet now. Wet and gooey. The lips of her vagina slid away. Her clitoris melted on Anthony's face and her liquid ass ran down the top of his head. The burning pain was unbearable, unending. He felt his face and scalp blistering. He could smell his torso cooking where it was in contact with Betty's bubbling, dripping body.

The last thing Anthony saw before a glob of Betty's ass fell and melted his eyeballs was a view past her pelvic bones, through her bare, sticky rib cage to where his cock was clutched between the teeth of her naked skull.

Then his eyes bubbled.

And Betty bit down.

Hard.

# NOODLERS NAB NEKKID NYMPHS

I've lived in Oklahoma all my life. I was born here and I reckon someday I'll die and they'll drop me into a red-dirt grave. While I've still got the ability to walk around, though, I enjoy exploring my home state. I've seen some pretty strange stuff over the years, but nothing really compares to the story I was told last summer when I went down to fish the Glover River in the Ouachita National Forest. I met a guy we'll call Bruce, and this is the story he told me as we sat on a sandbar a little apart from his companions, watching the moon rise and sail over the tops of the trees.

\* \* \*

I guess it all kinda started as we was coming up the road back there. I had a beer in one hand and was holding the steering wheel of my old truck with the other. It was my idea to come to the river today and do some noodlin'. Hot day like today drives those big catfish into their shady hidey-holes, you know. That makes noodlin' for them all that much easier. The heat was sure making things unpleasant in the cab of my truck. Donnie and Jeff were beginning to smell positively ripe.

I remember Donnie complaining, saying, "Dammit Bruce, why the fuck dontcha git rid of this piece-a-shit Chevy and get ya a truck with a fuckin air conditioner?" He's always been a Ford man.

Jeff said, "Yer just pissed cause yer monkey in the middle." He was sittin' on the passenger side. He said, "You don't like how Bruce's hand is hoverin over yer little dick as he changes gears."

We go back and forth like that all the time. Donnie, he said, "Bruce grabs his own dick enough, I don't want him gittin hold a mine. But damn! It's fuckin hot in here."

I guess it's all kinda dumb, but I wasn't about to be left out. I said, "I only grab my dick when yore mama ain't around to do it for me." I remember glancing away from the dirt road to look at them for a minute as I said it. It's true my Chevy pickup was an antique way before Garth Brooks had his first hit song, but as long as it's running I don't see any reason to trade it in on something newer.

Jeff, he wasn't ready to let the cut-downs stop. He said, "Ah shit, man, his mama ain't no good in bed."

"Fuck you," Donnie said. "At least her pussy gets wet. Yer mama has to smear lard on her twat just to let me in."

"That's cause you don't excite her with that little prick," Jeff said.

That's when I saw the yuppie truck. I yelled something like, "Fuckin she-iiiiit!" I dropped my beer bottle and grabbed the steering wheel hard with both hands while I ground the brake pedal to the floor.

My pickup skidded on the dirt road. Donnie shot forward and smashed his head on the windshield. The glass cracked and he fell back into his seat, dropping his beer. It glugged out all over the floor of my cab.

Donnie took off his Skoal cap and rubbed his forehead, then looked at the windshield. "Oh man, that fuckin hurts," he moaned.

I asked him if he was okay. I didn't see any blood leaking from under his fingers, but I made him move his hand so I could look.

"Maybe that crack'll let in some air," Jeff said.

I told him to shut up. Donnie parted his greasy hair and lowered his head. There was a red bump just above his forehead, but it didn't look too serious. "You'll live," I told him. "But you broke my fuckin windshield, ya shit."

"Your windshield about broke my fuckin head open," Donnie told me. He rubbed that knot on his head a little longer, then put his hat back on. "I gotta bump the size of Jeff's mama's tit on my head now. And what the fuck is that?" He pointed ahead of us.

I told him it was one of them Land Rovers. A yuppie SUV.

You probably saw it when you came in. It's a dark gray truck, half off the road and crashed into a thick elm tree. The front end of that sissified vehicle is wrapped around the tree and both the front doors are open. Wasn't anyone around, though.

"Who you think was drivin that?" Jeff asked.

"Fuck if I know, but you can bet it wasn't no one we know," I told him. "I don't know anybody'd drive a faggot truck like that."

"Maybe the cannibals got 'em," Jeff said. "People's always saying there's cannibals back here in these woods. You know, people what eats other people."

"Yeah, and fuckin Bigfoot lives down by Idabell, too," I said. "Maybe he parties with the cannibals."

"Would you fuck Bigfoot? If you found a woman one?" Jeff asked.

Jeff was always asking stupid shit like that. I told him to shut up, then I asked, "Where you think them people are? The ones that drove it down here?"

"Who cares?" Donnie said. "Prolly some damn city people came out here to buy their meth where the neighbors can't see 'em. Or maybe they're bird-watchin. Fuck 'em. We're almost to the fishin hole. Let's just go on. Fuck 'em, and their Land Rover, whoever they are."

"Yeah man, fuck 'em," Jeff echoed.

Since Jeff's mama wasn't around, I agreed. "Yeah, fuck 'em," I said. We rattled another half-mile up the dirt road, through them heavy woods, to that spot back there behind the trees. You saw the truck. Donnie and Jeff grabbed the cooler out of the back and I brought the lawn chairs.

The sunlight had turned the gray water into a sparkling silver streak. Insects were buzzing over the tall grass and birds were singing in the trees. It was a normal day, ya know. My dad used to bring me and Donnie here as kids. Jeff, he's two years younger. He started joining us after his family moved down the street from us back in junior high.

My dad gave us our first taste of beer here at the river. He told us the facts of life one day as we watched our bobbers bounce on the water. Then one day, Dad and my Uncle Jim set out to go fishing and they never came home.

I'd heard the cannibal stories – and the Bigfoot stories – and knew they were just so much bullshit. What's a fact, though, is that lots of folks come out to the forest here to grow their pot. Those folks defend their gardens with shotguns. Just about everyone around here knows someone who's been shot at for messing around on the wrong pot farm. It's usually city folks, like you, getting shot at, but sometimes locals find themselves in a bad place, too. The sheriff, he figured that's what happened to Dad and Uncle Jim.

But anyway, by the time I unfolded the first lawn chair, Donnie was already down to his skivvies.

"Bacon stripe!" Jeff hollered, pointing at the shit stain on the ass of Donnie's underwear.

"Yer mama's tongue got tired," Donnie said. "How's this?" He pulled the underwear off and threw them over with the rest of his clothes.

I told him, "Ain't no catfish gonna bite on that little worm. And my mama wouldn't, neither, so don't even fuckin say it." We're always ragging on someone's mama.

Jeff told me, "She'd have to fight yer sister away from it, anyway." Then he pulled off his own shirt.

I asked Donnie why we kept bringing that little shit out here with us. Meaning Jeff, of course.

"Fuck if I know," Donnie said. "I remember we used to let him drink our beer 'cause he'd steal Hustlers outta the quick shop, but since he got busted and his mama whipped his ass he don't do that no more. I don't know why we keep him around."

"You keep me around because yer jealous of my big pecker," Jeff said. He pointed at Donnie's little dick while he said it. I gotta admit, for a skinny little guy, Jeff had the biggest dick of all of us.

Donnie was about to get pissed, so I changed the subject. I asked, "Who's got the club?" Ya can't noodle without a club. Gotta beat the damn fish once ya git it up here.

Jeff said he'd get one, and he went off into the woods.

Donnie was already in the water, so I sat down to watch him for a bit. He waded upstream from a big sandbar and started feeling around under the bank with his arms. After just a couple of minutes, he started whooping. But then the fish that had him jerked his head under the water. I jumped up and ran to help him.

Donnie's legs were thrashing around and he was churning up mud and making the river water even murkier than it already was. I grabbed him by the waist and pulled. He came outta there faster than I expected. Knocked me down in hip-deep water and Donnie's ass hit me square in the face. Fuck, that was nasty. I pushed him away and he went over sideways.

There was a big flathead catfish on his arm. It'd clamped down on him all the way up to his elbow and was fighting like a woman dragging a man to the altar. I jumped up and grabbed the back of the fish, careful to keep from getting sliced open by the thrashing fins. That ever happen to you? Hurts like a motherfucker. I yelled at Donnie to get the fish on the sandbar.

"I'm fuckin tryin ta git him on the fuckin sand," Donnie screamed. His voice was as shrill as a little girl's. I swear to God.

We wrassled that big fish – at least an eighty-pounder – onto the sandbar. It flopped around, pulling some skin off

Donnie's arm and he was yelling and cussing, trying to get his arm outta that cat's mouth. "Where's Jeff and the fuckin club?" he kept asking.

Then I heard Jeff screaming. I looked over the top of the riverbank and saw him running out of the woods. He was screaming like a little girl that'd seen a rat the size of a goat. He was waving his arms and yelling, "Get in the fuckin' truck! He's got a knife and he wants my dick!"

Then this other guy comes running outta the woods after Jeff. He was a slender guy, not more than a hundred-fifty pounds, with wild black hair and wide, crazy eyes. He was wearing khaki pants and a yellow Polo shirt that was all stained up with mud and grass. Hell, you saw him laying over there by the bank. I was sure the fucker came from that Land Rover. The yuppie had a filet knife in one fist and was catching up to Jeff.

Donnie got that fish off his arm about then and stood up so he could see.

"Reckon Jeff fucked that feller's wife?" I asked.

"Mebbe. Or his dog," Donnie said. Jeff was a horny son of a bitch, but I don't think he ever fucked a dog.

"We better help him out," I said, and I started climbing up the bank. Donnie slipped as he tried to climb up behind me and I had to stop and pull him up.

Well, that yuppie caught Jeff and dragged him down. He straddled Jeff's chest, facing his feet, and started cutting away his jeans with that filet knife. I couldn't fucking believe what I was seeing.

I yelled, "Let'im go, you dumbass!" and charged across the fifty yards separating us from Jeff and the crazy guy. The yuppie ignored me and kept slicing at Jeff's jeans and underwear.

"Get him off me!" Jeff was screaming over and over. "Get the fucker off me!"

The stranger had hold of Jeff's dick and was stretching it out like a piece of taffy or something. I told ya Jeff had a big dick, right? Anyway, I screamed, "Don't do it!" but I was still too far away. I saw the blood squirt as the knife slid through the bottom part of Jeff's dick. Jeff screamed like one of them opera stars then.

I was close enough by then I just threw myself at that crazy fucking yuppie bastard. I remember slamming into the little guy's chest and knocking him off Jeff. We rolled around in the grass, but I couldn't get a hold on him.

The yuppie got up first. He was holding his knife in one hand and Jeff's dripping dick in the other. His eyes ... man, they was burning like some kind of sick animal. He held up Jeff's dick and said, "I'll get my own perfect woman now!" I swear that's what he said. Then he turned around and ran for the river.

I wasn't sure what to do. Go after the guy, or help Jeff. I mean, Jeff was laying there with blood pumping out of a hole where his dick used to be.

"Get him, man," Donnie yelled, finally getting his ass over to us. "Maybe the doctor can sew it back on."

I jumped up and hurried after the city fuck. He'd lost a loafer as he ran back to the river, but didn't seem to care. I got to him just as he cocked his arm to throw Jeff's dick. I grabbed the fucker and slung him around, but it was too late. I saw Jeff's big dick flying through the air, then it splashed into the river and was gone.

I threw the yuppie fuck down, then kicked him in the face once or twice. The guy tried to roll away, but when he did he rolled over his knife. I swear I didn't kill him. When he rolled onto his back, the handle of the filet knife was sticking out of his chest. He twitched a couple of times, then just died. It was creepy watching the wildness fade outta his crazy eyes. Then he just laid there with a blank stare, like he was looking at the clear blue sky.

"Ho-lee fucking she-it," Donnie said, coming over to where I was.

Bugs were still buzzing and birds were still singing, but otherwise the place seemed really quiet after all that screaming.

I told Donnie, "Jeff's pecker's gone."

"Long gone," Donnie agreed. "Jeff passed out. The pain, I guess. Mebbe shock."

We went back over to Jeff. Blood was still leaking from the hole in his crotch.

"Shit man, it's like he's got a pussy and it's that time a the month," Donnie said.

I told him, "He could be fuckin dyin, man." Then I sent him to get his shirt wet and come back so we could clean Jeff up and see if we could get the bleeding to stop.

I knelt down beside Jeff. He was really pale, like a ghost. I said something like, "Shit, Jeff. I'm sorry, man. Yer gonna be okay, though. We'll get this bleedin slowed down and get you back to a doctor." I was gonna say more, but Donnie interrupted me.

"Ho-lee she-it!" he said again.

I turned around to see what he was talking about this time. Donnie was standing at the riverbank, looking down at the water. I went over to see what was going on.

There was a naked woman standing thigh-deep in the sparkling water, just looking back at us. She had long, wavy blonde hair, tits like beach balls, and I'm just damn sure she'd shaved her bush. It was a perfect, narrow little triangle. You saw her. Hell, what am I telling you for. Her lips were painted red as cherries and her eye shadow was turquoise, like good Indian jewelry. She didn't have a tan line or cottage cheese cellulose wrinkle anywhere on that perfect body. She had a 12-pack of Budweiser in one hand and a giant bag of pork rinds in the other. She waded to the sandbar and stood looking down at the catfish for a minute, then looked up at us again. Her voice was all sweet and pouty.

"How ya'll boys doin?" she asked, shifting her chest to show off her giant knockers.

"Where'd you come from?" I asked.

"Outta the river," she said. "I's just waitin fer sumbuddy ta throw a willy in the water so's I could be born."

I asked her, "You mean ... yer made outta Jeff's dick?"

"That's right," she said, smiling. "Name's Daisy."

"Ho-lee she-it," Donnie said again.

Donnie'd done popped a boner just looking at the woman. His little dick was pointing right at her. I gotta admit I could already feel some stirring in my own pants. I asked her, "Whatcha want?"

She stroked the glistening green back of the dead catfish with a toe. "I want ya'll ta come down here and party with me," she said, hefting the beer and rinds.

I asked her, "Why can'tcha come up here?"

"I can't leave the riverbed," she said. "Them's the rules. Ya'll have to come down here."

Donnie, he was already scrambling off the bank and onto the sandbar. He stood in front of Daisy, looking from her tits to the beer, back to her tits, then at the pork rinds and finally back to her tits. He asked, "They any more like you in there?" and nodded over her shoulder to the river.

"Lots," she said. "They just need a little help bein born."

"Did ya fucking hear that?" he asked, looking back at me. Then his eyes got real big and he jumped back up the bank and ran to that dead yuppie. He jerked the guy's pants down to his knees, then plucked the filet knife outta his chest.

"What're you doin?" I yelled.

Donnie ignored me and reached for the guy's dick with his free hand. He seemed to hesitate a second, like he didn't really wanna touch another guy's dick, but then he grabbed it, pulled it up like a piece of putty and sliced it away.

I couldn't believe it. Then I remembered I was alone with Daisy. I hauled my ass out to the sandbar to keep her company. "How bout givin me one a them brews?" I asked. She offered me a beer, and it was ice cold. I popped it open and took a big drink. It was the sweetest beer I've ever had, and I'm usually a Coors man.

"I'll give ya the pork rinds, too, but ya gotta hump me first," Daisy said.

I told her, "I sure as hell reckon I can do that." I stripped off my clothes while she put the beer and rinds down. She sprawled out on the sandbar with her feet still in the water, so I dropped between her open legs and was just about ready to poke her when Donnie jumped off the bank. Fucker splashed into the river with the yuppie's dick leaking blood all over his hand.

"Looka this," he yelled, then threw the pecker in the river. We watched the meat splash and disappear. A minute or so later this brunette came outta the waves. She came up to the shore, her hair and body already dry. "Oh, hot damn!" Donnie said. He was damn near dancing with joy.

I couldn't believe what I just saw. I think I said, "Fuck me runnin."

You probably didn't get a good look at her since Donnie was humping her again when you walked up. Her tits are as big and firm as her hips are wide. When she came outta the water she had a NASCAR trophy in one hand and a bottle of Jack Daniel's in the other. Her lips and fingernails were fire engine red and her eyes were like drops of moist chocolate. Man, she looked sweet.

"Looka them *hips*," Donnie yelled. "I'll ride that doggy *all* fuckin night!" He ran out to meet her.

"You gonna hump me or what?" Daisy asked me. "Luanne'll keep yer friend busy."

Well, of course I did. I kept telling myself over and over I was humping on a woman and not something made out of Jeff's dick. It was kinda freaky to think of it the other way.

Out in the river, Donnie took Luanne standing up, not that it took him very long to finish. They was done and wading back toward the sandbar about the time I finished.

"Wooo, shit!" Donnie said as they came up. He was taking swigs from the whiskey bottle. "That's some good pussy. Maybe we can swap later, huh?"

"All right with me," I said. "Fuckin made me hungry. Let's grill some of this cat."

61

Donnie said he'd go get the li'l barbecue outta the truck. We always bring it so we can cook the fish. He started back up the bank, but all of a sudden he stopped and doubled over. He made a funny choking noise, then started puking up river water. When he turned around, his face was all bloated and starting to kind of fall apart around the eyes and mouth. It was some weird-ass shit.

"What the fuck's wrong with you?" I asked. I told him I didn't want him puking on my grill and that I'd get the damn thing myself. I climbed up the bank and suddenly I started puking river water, too. It flew out of my mouth so hard it hit the dirt and splashed back up in my face. I put my hands in front of my mouth to keep from puking again, and that's when I saw that my fingers were all pale and bloated up like a bunch of drowned worms. Donnie's hands looked the same.

We turned around and looked at them women. We knew it was their fault.

Daisy, she tore a strip of meat off that big catfish and sucked on it, looking back at us and smiling, all innocent-like.

"Ya dinnit think our pussies was free, didcha?" Luanne asked. "We can't leave the riverbed, and now you can't, neither. Come on back down here fore ya drown."

I shoulda known there's no such thing as a free fuck. I still had river water running down my chin and I could feel that my face was all puffy. I looked from the women to the trees there, wondering if I could make a run for my truck. Then I looked over and saw Jeff, marinated in his own blood and baking in the hot sun.

I think I said, "Fuckin shit ain't right." Something like that. Then my stomach gurgled and more water exploded outta my mouth and nose. My muscles felt all rubbery and weak. I groaned like I was dying, then crawled back to the riverbank and slid down it to the water. As soon as my hand broke the surface of the river, my body was back to normal and I felt fine.

Donnie rolled down the bank beside me and went right into the river. When he got up he was back to normal, too. "Shit, Bruce, what the hell's goin on?" he asked me.

I ignored him and asked the women, "So, long as we stay down here with you, we're okay? But we go up there and we look like we done drowned and we spew this nasty river water all the time?"

"Yup," Daisy answered. "You *will* drown if ya stay up there. Wouldn't that look funny? Drownin on dry land like that?"

"Fuck me runnin," I said again. "This shit ain't right."

"Listen man," Donnie said, all serious-like. "We got nekkid wimmin, beer, whiskey, rinds and a fuckin NASCAR trophy. Maybe it ain't so bad. I always wanted one of those trophies."

"This shit ain't right," I said again. Then I asked the women, "Ya'll got anything else you wanna tell us? Woulda been nice if you'd told us we wouldn't be able to leave the river before we fucked ya."

"Well, there is one thing," Luanne said. "When the sun comes up tomorrow, we'll have to eat you."

Needless to say, I was a little pissed.

"Them's the rules," Daisy agreed. "But until then we'll do anything ya want. You'll be smilin' right up to the end."

Donnie asked, "You'll do anything? Even …" I don't know what he was thinking. Probably something about ass-fucking. He was always saying how he wanted to try that.

Luanne came over to stand beside me. I guess she saw I didn't like the idea of being eaten. "Anything," she said. "Anything you want."

Donnie said, "Fuckin'-A!"

It was like he hadn't heard the downside. I yelled, "Did you hear that, dumbass? She said they're gonna *eat* us. I don't think they mean that in the blowjob kind of way. We're fucking gonna die over a piece of ass. Us and Jeff."

"And he ain't even getting' any," Donnie laughed. "I say, if we're gonna go, let's make it good. I always said if I had to go I wanted to be fucked to death. Didn't I say that?"

I ignored him. Luanne put a hand under my chin and made me look her in the face. She said, "You look awful familiar. Did yer daddy used to fish here?"

So, that's it. The sun'll be up soon. I can't leave the river, so I'm gonna get one more good humping in before ... you know. Before they eat us. They done stripped the meat off that catfish. I ain't looking forward to that. Hopefully they'll kill us first.

I told you all this shit because I want you to call my mom and tell her what happened. Tell her what happened to me, and to Dad. She thought he ran off with another woman. She never did believe he got shot for trespassing. I guess, in a way, she was right all along. Except she'd never believe he got eaten by a woman that came outta the river.

\* \* \*

That said, Bruce went back downstream and a few minutes later I heard a woman moaning with pleasure. I thought about sticking around to see the end, but decided

I really didn't want to know if those women were going to eat Bruce and Donnie. Jeff and the city guy were both dead, so I got out of the woods to a place where my cell phone would work and called the sheriff.

That's one part of the state I don't plan to return to any time soon.

# ABOUT THE AUTHOR

Steven E. Wedel lives in central Oklahoma with his wife and most of his kids ... the ones who haven't grown up enough to leave the den yet, anyway. He began writing in the mid-1980s and has kept at it despite numerous disappointments and setbacks. Steve has a bachelor's degree in journalism from the University of Central Oklahoma and a master's degree in liberal studies from the University of Oklahoma. He has worked as a machinist, bookseller, stock clerk, journalist, public relations specialist and is now a high school English teacher most of the year.

Visit him online at www.stevenewedel.com.

.